Cold Whispers II

TERROR in the UNDERGROUND TUNNEL

by Dee Phillips

illustrated by Timo Grubing

BEARPORT
PUBLISHING

New York, New York

Credits

Cover, © Claudiodivizia/Dreamstime and © Elzbieta Sekowska/Shutterstock.

Publisher: Kenn Goin
Senior Editor: Joyce Tavolacci
Creative Director: Spencer Brinker

Library of Congress Cataloging-in-Publication in process at time of publication (2017)
Library of Congress Control Number: 2016018785
ISBN-13: 978-1-944102-37-1 (library binding)

For more information, write to Bearport Publishing Company, Inc.,
45 West 21st Street, Suite 3B, New York, New York 10010.
Printed in the United States of America.

10 9 8 7 6 5 4 3 2 1

Contents

CHAPTER 1

The Abandoned Subway

Emma and David had just had a great day visiting Buckingham Palace and the Tower of London with their mom. Now the day was about to get even better. They were in the back of a shiny black London taxi on their way to their mom's movie **shoot** in an **abandoned** subway station.

Having a famous movie **director** for a mom wasn't always fun. She was often away from home for weeks at a time. But, on this occasion, Emma and David got to join her in London. The taxi pulled up to the entrance of the old subway station and mom's **assistant**, Elly, opened the car door.

"Hi, guys," said Elly. "Welcome to the London Underground!"

"Thanks, Elly," said Emma and David's mom. Then she rushed off to meet with the other members of the movie **crew**.

"Come with me," said Elly as she led the kids into the subway station. "I've got some chairs ready for you so you can watch all the action."

"How old is this place?" asked Emma as she looked around, careful not to bump into any of the huge cameras and large, blinding spotlights.

"This station was built about a hundred and fifty years ago," said Elly. "And it's been closed up for thirty years or so."

"What's down there?" asked David. He pointed to an old staircase that seemed to go on forever.

"Right now, we're standing in the ticket office," said Elly. "The stairs lead down to the **platforms** and the tunnels, which are about one hundred feet below ground."

"Awesome!" said David.

"Many sections of the London Underground are now abandoned," continued Elly. "It's kind of creepy to think there's a **labyrinth** of empty passageways and tunnels deep below the city."

Elly pointed to two seats. Emma and David settled into the chairs as the movie crew **frantically** scurried around them.

"I want to see the tunnels," whispered Emma to her brother.

"We're supposed to stay here," David whispered back. Secretly, though, he was curious, too.

"Come on," said Emma. "Let's just take a quick look around. Mom won't notice that we're gone."

Everyone in the old ticket office was watching the actors at work as Emma and David slipped away down the long set of stairs leading to the **deserted** tunnels.

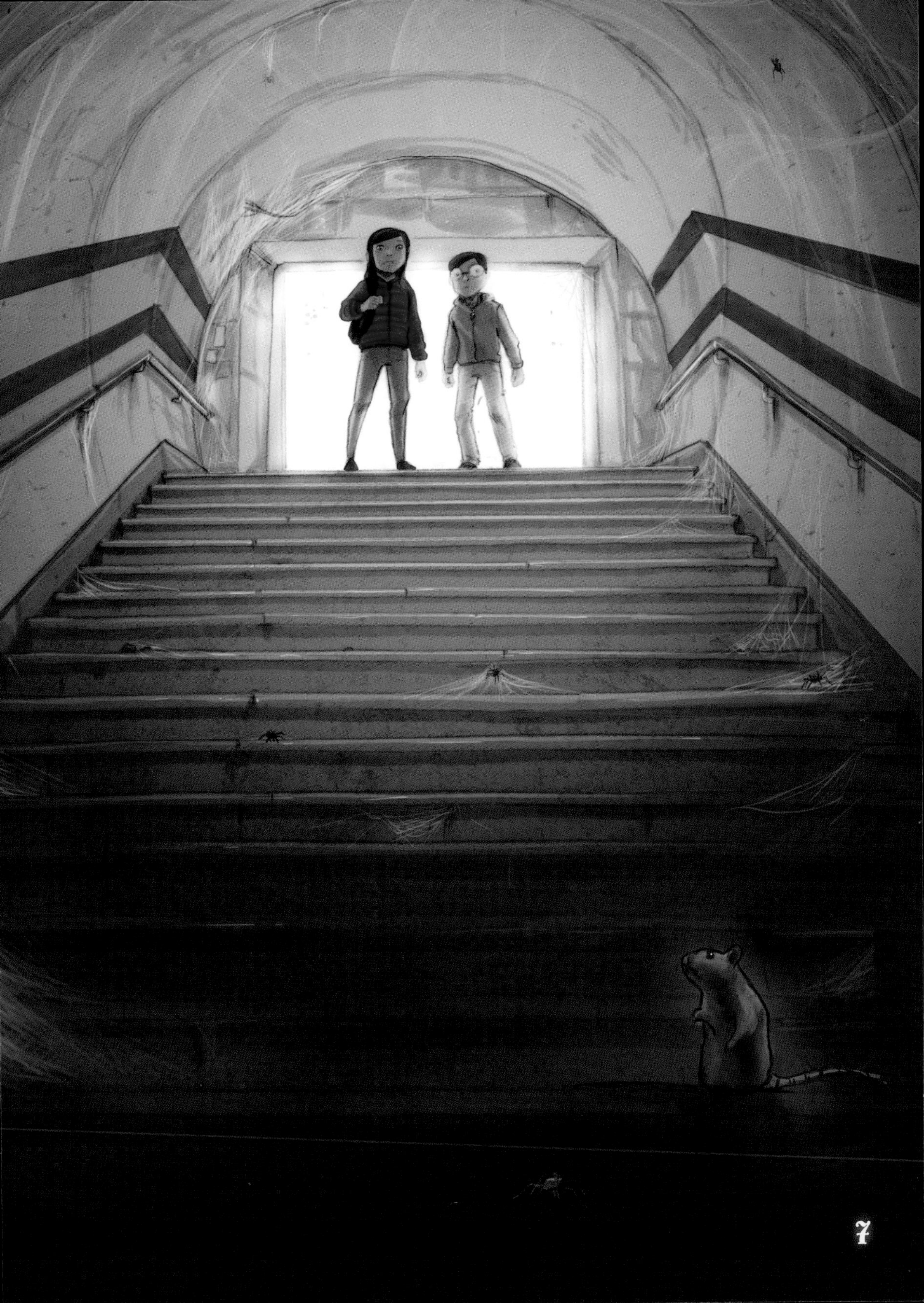

CHAPTER 2

The Voice in the Labyrinth

At the bottom of the stairs, Emma and David found themselves in a gloomy tunnel that was once used as a walkway for subway passengers. Old lights flickered above them and made an unsettling buzzing sound. The tunnel had a rounded ceiling, and the walls were covered with green- and cream-colored tiles.

"Come on," said Emma.

They walked quickly along the tunnel. It twisted and turned from left to right. David shivered a little as he thought of Elly's description of the subway as a labyrinth.

Suddenly, they found themselves at the top of another steep set of stairs.

Emma grabbed the rusty metal handrail and headed down the steps. David followed.

All of a sudden, Emma froze. There was something

moving in the dark shadows at the bottom of the stairs.

"Who's there?" she called out.

David felt as if hundreds of tiny bugs were crawling down his spine.

In fearful silence, Emma and David hesitated. Then a tiny mouse bolted across the bottom stair.

They breathed a sigh of **relief** and hurried down the remaining stairs. They found themselves in another passenger tunnel.

This deeper tunnel was even gloomier. In many places, the tiles were missing from the damp, stained walls.

"Do you think we're a hundred feet underground yet?" said David.

"Maybe," said Emma.

The only sounds were their feet moving along the crumbling concrete floor and water dripping slowly from the ceiling.

Then out of nowhere, they heard a noise. It was a low rumbling sound coming from somewhere ahead. The rumble grew louder and louder. Then they heard the metallic screeching of a train's brakes.

Emma looked at her brother, confused. "There's a train down here?" she said.

"That's not possible," said David. "The station has been closed for a long time."

"Come on," shouted Emma. "I want to find the train." But she was too late. The sound of the train began to fade away.

That's when they heard the voice.

"Mama. Please come back, Mama."

It was the high-pitched cry of a small child. The voice floated along the tunnel. Emma and David had no idea what direction it was coming from.

The child began to sob. "Please come back, Mama. I'm all alone."

"Oh no!" exclaimed David. "Maybe a little kid got lost down here."

"I think the voice is coming from up ahead," said Emma. "Let's go!"

Emma and David began to run. Suddenly, the tunnel opened up into a large cavern-like space. They found themselves on a station platform. At either end of the platform were dark, gaping holes that led to a train tunnel.

At the far end of the platform, they saw a little girl. Her curly hair was tied with a large white bow. She was wearing a short summer dress that was dirty and torn. Her shoulders shook as she sobbed. "Please come back, Mama. I'm all alone," she cried.

Emma and David walked slowly toward the little girl.

"Hi," said Emma softly. "My name's Emma. What's your name?"

The child turned around to look at them. Emma gasped. In the child's tear-stained face were the strangest eyes she'd ever seen. They were totally black.

The little girl then looked sadly into the dark train tunnel. "Please come back, Mama," she said.

"Are you lost?" Emma asked. She realized her voice sounded shaky. "How did you get down here?"

Emma crouched down so her eyes were level with the child's black, glassy eyes. "My name is Emma," she said again. "And this is my brother, David."

This time, the little girl said nothing.

Emma shivered. It was cold on the station platform, and

the child was wearing only a thin dress.

"Are you cold?" asked Emma. She slipped her backpack from her shoulders and began to look inside for a sweater.

Suddenly, the little girl smiled. She pointed to the front of Emma's backpack. Peeking out of the bag was a small teddy bear that Emma had bought as a **souvenir** at the Tower of London. Emma handed the bear to the little girl.

Then the child pointed to the bag again."That's pretty," she said with a smile.

Just visible in the backpack was Emma's cellphone. It had a pale blue cover decorated with glitter.

"Here, I'll take your picture." Emma held up the phone to the girl's face and clicked. All the little kids that Emma knew loved to have their photos taken.

"Let's go, Em," said David, pleading. "This is weird. How did this little girl get down here? We need to tell someone and get help."

Emma reached for the little girl's hand, but she backed away. Sobs began to shake her tiny body again.

"Mama. I want my mother!" she howled. Then she turned and ran along the platform.

"Come back!" Emma shouted. Suddenly, the child jumped from the platform onto the shadowy train tracks and started running. Soon, the outline of her body blended into the blackness of the train tunnel.

"Come on!" said Emma. "We have to go after her."

"No, wait. We should find Mom and tell her what happened," shouted David.

Emma looked down the tunnel and then turned to face her brother. "Okay, I guess you're right."

Emma grabbed her backpack, and they both began to run along the platform and back into the long passenger tunnel. They ran up the stairs and along the next tunnel. Gasping for breath, they climbed the final staircase into the brightly lit ticket office.

There they saw their mom, who was talking with Elly.

"Mom! Mom!" shouted Emma. "There's a little kid down there!" She pointed to the stairs behind her. "She's lost, and she ran into a tunnel, and we heard a train . . ."

Before Emma could continue, her mom interrupted her. "Where have you two been? And what on earth are you talking about? You know the station is abandoned."

"Look, Mom," Emma said, pulling her cellphone from her backpack. "I took a photo of the girl." Emma found the photo on her phone. Everything was just as they'd seen it. The gloomy, **dilapidated** platform. The train tracks. The tunnel. But there was no child. The little girl with the black eyes was nowhere to be seen!

"What? I can't believe it!" David looked at the photo. He sounded as confused as Emma felt.

Mom and Elly looked at the photo of the empty station platform, too.

"Okay, guys," said Mom. "Where's this mysterious little girl?"

"The crew has been working here for weeks getting the movie set ready. No one's been allowed down into that station," said Elly.

Mom turned to Emma and David, "I think it's been a really long day. You've had too much excitement. I think we all need a good night's sleep." Elly nodded her head in agreement.

Soon, they were all in the back of a taxi heading to their hotel. As their mom and Elly chatted and checked e-mails, Emma and David stared at the photo.

"I just don't understand," whispered Emma to her brother. "We definitely saw that little girl."

"Do you think she was real? I mean . . . was she . . . could she have been . . ." David's voice trailed off.

Emma stared out of the taxi window at the dark London streets and thought about the twisting, turning tunnels of the Underground beneath them. Was a small child lost down there? Was there anything she and David could do to help?

CHAPTER 3

A Deadly Journey

The next morning, David felt exhausted. During the night, each time he tried to fall asleep, he saw the little girl's haunting black eyes and tear-stained face.

At breakfast, between mouthfuls of cereal, Emma told David, "We have to go back down there."

David was silent for a long time. "Are you sure?" he said as his stomach churned with fear and concern.

"We can't leave that little girl all alone," said Emma. "Let's tell Mom we want to go to work with her again."

"I guess you're right," said David reluctantly.

A few hours later, they were back at the subway station. Mom gave them strict instructions not to go wandering off. Emma and David knew that soon all the adults would be **absorbed** in their work, and they could easily creep away when no one was watching.

Emma and David waited for the right moment and then hurried down the stairs and through the Underground's tunnels. As they walked, David wondered, *Who was that little girl? Had it all been a dream?*

Then, just before they reached the station platform, they heard a familiar sound. A child's sobs echoed through the tunnel.

"It's the little girl again," whispered Emma. "See, we didn't imagine it!"

Trying not to make a sound, they crept to the end of the tunnel and out onto the platform.

The little girl was standing on the very edge, staring into the dark train tunnel. She was hugging the teddy bear close to her trembling little body.

"Hello, again," said Emma softly.

The little girl continued to stare into the tunnel. "Mama will be here soon," she said.

"What do you mean?" asked Emma.

The little girl wiped her eyes and smiled. "The train will be here soon. Will you help me get on it? Please help me. The door is really heavy."

"Em!" hissed David. "Listen."

They could hear a rumbling sound coming from the tunnel. The little girl jumped up and down. "It's coming! It's coming!" she cried.

A wave of icy, dusty air burst out of the tunnel. Then a shiny, red train screeched to a halt alongside the platform. It looked like something from an old movie. The gold lettering on its side sparkled, and its windows were spotless.

The little girl ran to one of the train doors. Her voice became more **insistent**. "Mama! Mama!" she cried. "Don't leave. Don't leave." She looked over her shoulder at Emma and David. "Please help me get on!"

Emma ran to the door and pulled hard on the handle. The door to the train slid open.

The little girl excitedly grabbed Emma's hand and pulled her onto the train. "Come on!" she shouted.

"Emma, where are you going?" cried David. Before he could wrap his head around what was happening, he darted onto the train behind Emma and the little girl. Then the doors shut tightly behind them.

The train jolted and moved forward. As it sped down the tracks, it jerked from side to side.

The little girl ran through the train car as Emma and David followed her. Emma looked at the shiny chestnut-colored wood inside the train. The plush, padded seats were covered with red checkered fabric that looked like a chessboard.

At the far end of the carriage, a young woman was standing. She looked like a character from one of their mom's movies that takes place in the past.

The woman knelt down and the little girl rushed into her arms.

"Mama! Mama!" sobbed the little child. "I missed you so much!"

"Oh! My darling little Betty!" cried the young woman. "It's been so long. Finally, you've come back to me."

Then the woman looked up at Emma and David. David's stomach flipped over with fear. The woman had the same black eyes as the little girl.

"Thank you!" the woman gasped. "Thank you for bringing my Betty back to me."

Suddenly, the woman's **expression** changed from joy to misery. She seemed panicked and afraid.

"You have to get off the train!" she cried. "You have to get off before it's too late!"

The train began to shake more violently as it barreled down the tunnel. Emma and David grabbed a pole to steady themselves. Outside, the walls of the tunnel flashed by, faster and faster.

Before Emma and David could ask why they had to exit the train, the carriage filled with the terrible noise of screeching brakes. Then there was a **deafening** crash and the sound of crunching metal.

That's when Emma and David felt themselves being flung through the air.

Emma smashed into the end of the carriage. David's head connected hard with a metal rail as smoke filled the air.

Then nothing. Just blackness . . . and silence.

CHAPTER 4

A Ghost in the Underground?

"Em? Em? Oh my gosh. Are you okay?" cried David as he shook Emma's shoulders.

Emma was lying on the ground and slowly opened her eyes.

"I think we're on the train tracks," said David.

Suddenly, they could hear voices shouting. "David! Emma! Hello! Are you there?" Then beams of flashlights broke through the darkness. It was their mom, Elly, some guys from the movie crew, and a police officer.

Their mom looked very upset. "Are you okay? What happened to you two?" she shouted.

The adults helped Emma and David to their feet.

"We found the little girl," Emma said, still stunned from the crash. "We got on the train with her."

"What are you talking about, Em?" asked Elly.

"She's right," said David. He fought to hold back tears. "We were on a train. Then it crashed. They must be here somewhere. The little girl and her mother. They might still be alive." David swallowed down a big sob.

"No trains have been down here for years," said the police officer. "I've been working in the Underground for three decades, and this station has been empty all that time."

"I do recall that there was once a huge crash in this tunnel," he said, becoming more **somber**. "It was a long time ago . . . in 1938. A **signal** broke and two trains collided. One of the trains caught fire. It was one of the worst subway accidents on record."

He shined his flashlight up the tunnel wall. "Look," he said. "You can still see **scorch** marks from the fire on the wall."

27

"Was anybody hurt?" asked David. He didn't recognize his own voice. It sounded shaky and weak.

"Yes," said the officer. "Mostly businesspeople on their way home from work. But there was a young woman and her daughter on the train, too. They say the mother was killed instantly. The little girl was found wandering in the tunnel calling for her mother."

Emma and David froze.

"The little girl was taken to the hospital and died later that night," said the police officer. "Her name was . . ."

"Her name was Betty!" gasped Emma, interrupting the police officer. "We saw the little girl. She was trying to get back to her mother. Mom, we told you about her last night! We told you!"

The police officer said, "You wouldn't be the first to think you'd seen a ghost in the London Underground."

David took his sister's hand and squeezed it. His face said, *No one's ever going to believe us.*

As they walked back along the tunnel, the adults talked.

"*Spooky old tunnels. . . . So many stories of ghosts down here. . . .*"

Emma's foot suddenly hit something soft on the train tracks. She bent down and picked it up.

"David, look!" she said.

It was a small teddy bear. Its body was crushed and its clothes were torn.

"It's the bear I gave to Betty," said Emma.

"What happened to it?" asked David.

Emma gently brushed ash and black soot from the bear's soft yellow fur.

"I'm not sure," she said, looking deeply into her brother's eyes. "It looks as if it's been in a fiery crash."

WHAT DO YOU THINK?

Terror in the Underground Tunnel

1. Why are Emma and David visiting an abandoned subway station in London?

2. Who is the little girl on the platform waiting for?

3. Why are Emma and David confused when they look at this photo on Emma's cell phone?

4. What emotions do you think Emma and David feel when they find the small, scorched teddy bear on the train tracks at the end of the story?

5. Do you think this story has a happy or sad ending? Explain your thoughts.

GLOSSARY

abandoned (uh-BAN-duhnd)
no longer in use

absorbed (ab-ZORBD)
intensely engaged

assistant (uh-SISS-tuhnt)
a person who helps someone
do a job

crew (KROO) a team of
people who work together

deafening (DEF-uh-ning)
impossible to hear anything

deserted (di-ZUR-tid) empty;
having no people in an area

dilapidated (dih-LAP-ih-day-tid)
fallen into disrepair or ruin

director (duh-REK-tur)
a person who manages the people
who work on a movie

expression (ek-SPRESH-uhn)
the look on someone's face

frantically (FRAN-tik-lee) to
do something with worry or fear

insistent (in-SIS-tent)
demanding something

labyrinth (LAB-uh-rinth) a set
of winding, connected pathways
in which it is easy to get lost

platforms (PLAT-forms) the
raised structures along the side of
a railroad track where passengers
get on and off trains

relief (ri-LEEF) the feeling
of relaxation after something
stressful happens

scorch (SKORCH) to burn
the surface of something with fire

shoot (SHOOT) a place where
a movie is filmed

signal (SIG-nuhl) a message or
warning

somber (SOM-bur) dark and
gloomy or very sad

souvenir (soo-vuh-NEER) an
object you keep that reminds you
of a place, person, or event

ABOUT THE AUTHOR

Dee Phillips develops and writes nonfiction books for young readers and fiction books—including historical fiction—for middle grades and young adults. She loves to read and write stories that have a twist or an unexpected, thought-provoking ending. Dee lives near the ocean on the southwest coast of England. A keen hiker, her biggest ambition is to one day walk the entire coast of Great Britain.

ABOUT THE ILLUSTRATOR

German-based illustrator Timo Grubing works on children's books, educational books, and magazines. When he's not working on projects for children, he enjoys drawing zombie comics. He lives and works in Bochum, Germany, in the heart of the Ruhr area, with his girlfriend, who's also an illustrator, and two cats, which do not have artistic dispositions.